Roy on the Ranch

The Sound of R

by Cecilia Minden and Joanne Meier · illustrated by Bob Ostrom

The Child's World

Published by The Child's World®
1980 Lookout Drive
Mankato, MN 56003-1705
800-599-READ
www.childsworld.com

The Child's World®: Mary Berendes, Publishing Director
The Design Lab: Design and page production

Library of Congress Cataloging-in-Publication Data
Minden, Cecilia.
Roy on the ranch : the sound of R / by Cecilia Minden and Joanne Meier ; illustrated by Bob Ostrom.
p. cm.
ISBN 978-1-60253-415-5 (library bound : alk. paper)
1. English language–Consonants–Juvenile literature. 2. English language–Phonetics–Juvenile literature. 3. Reading–Phonetic method–Juvenile literature. I. Meier, Joanne D. II. Ostrom, Bob. III. Title.
PE1159.M57 2010
[E]–dc22 2010005606

Printed in the United States of America in Mankato, MN.
July 2010
F11538

NOTE TO PARENTS AND EDUCATORS:

The Child's World® has created this series with the goal of exposing children to engaging stories and illustrations that assist in phonics development. The books in the series will help children learn the relationships between the letters of written language and the individual sounds of spoken language. This contact helps children learn to use these relationships to read and write words.

The books in this series follow a similar format. An introductory page, to be read by an adult, introduces the child to the phonics feature, or sound, that will be highlighted in the book. Read this page to the child, stressing the phonic feature. Help the student learn how to form the sound with her mouth. The story and engaging illustrations follow the introduction. At the end of the story, word lists categorize the feature words into their phonic elements.

Each book in this series has been carefully written to meet specific readability requirements. Close attention has been paid to elements such as word count, sentence length, and vocabulary. Readability formulas measure the ease with which the text can be read and understood. Each book in this series has been analyzed using the Spache readability formula.

Reading research suggests that systematic phonics instruction can greatly improve students' word recognition, spelling, and comprehension skills. This series assists in the teaching of phonics by providing students with important opportunities to apply their knowledge of phonics as they read words, sentences, and text.

This is the letter r.

In this book, you will read words that have the **r** sound as in: *ranch, ride, river,* and *run.*

Roy lives on a ranch.

This is his horse, Big Red.

This is his dog, Rascal.

Roy rides Big Red around the ranch. They like to ride along the river.

Rascal runs beside Roy and Big Red.

Rascal likes to chase rabbits.
The rabbits run away.

Roy is learning to rope cattle.

It takes lots of practice!

It is starting to rain.

Roy will return to the ranch.

Pretend you live on a ranch.
What would you like to do?

Fun Facts

If you hear someone talking about a kitten, you might assume that person is referring to a baby cat. But did you know that baby rabbits are also called kittens? Male and female rabbits are called bucks and does. The same names are used to describe male and female deer. Like cats, some rabbits make excellent family pets. But like deer, other rabbits are better off in the wild. You might think that rabbits are cuddly and adorable, but many farmers do not like wild rabbits because they eat crops.

You probably have heard of people riding horses. How would you feel about riding a camel or an elephant? People in Asia and Africa sometimes ride these animals, but horseback riding is more common in the United States. Athletes ride horses in races or as part of a sport called *polo*.

Activity

Horseback or Pony Riding

Have you ever ridden a pony or a horse? Sometimes town fairs feature pony rides, or maybe there is a stable in your area that offers horseback-riding lessons. If you live near a local stable, ask your parents if you can visit and possibly speak with some of the people who work there. Before you ride a horse or pony, make sure you are comfortable around these animals and are familiar with important safety rules.

To Learn More

Books

About the Sound of R

Moncure, Jane Belk. *My "r" Sound Box®*. Mankato, MN: The Child's World, 2009.

About Rabbits

Rohmann, Eric. *My Friend Rabbit*. New York: Square Fish, 2002.

Swanson, Diane. *Welcome to the World of Rabbits and Hares*. Vancouver: Whitecap Books, 2000.

About Ranches

Munro, Roxie. *Ranch*. Albany, TX: Bright Sky Press, 2004.

Noble, Trinka Hakes, and Tony Ross (illustrator). *Meanwhile Back at the Ranch*. New York: Dial, 1987.

About Riding

DK Publishing. *Horse and Pony Pack: A Guide to Riding and Horse Care*. New York: Funfax, 1999.

Ransford, Sandy. *First Riding Lessons*. New York: Kingfisher, 2002.

Web Sites

Visit our home page for lots of links about the Sound of R:

childsworld.com/links

Note to Parents, Teachers, and Librarians: We routinely check our Web links to make sure they're safe, active sites—so encourage your readers to check them out!

R Feature Words

Proper Names

Rascal
Red
Roy

Feature Words in Initial Position

rabbit
rain
ranch
return
ride
river
rope
run

About the Authors

Cecilia Minden, PhD, is the former director of the Language and Literacy Program at the Harvard Graduate School of Education. She is now a reading consultant for school and library publications. She earned her PhD in reading education from the University of Virginia. Cecilia and her husband, Dave Cupp, live outside Chapel Hill, North Carolina. They enjoy sharing their love of reading with their grandchildren, Chelsea and Qadir.

Joanne Meier, PhD, has worked as an elementary school teacher, university professor, and researcher. She earned her BA in early childhood education from the University of South Carolina, and her MEd and PhD in education from the University of Virginia. She currently works as a literacy consultant for schools and private organizations. Joanne lives in Virginia with her husband Eric, daughters Kella and Erin, two cats, and a gerbil.

About the Illustrator

Bob Ostrom has been illustrating children's books for nearly twenty years. A graduate of the New England School of Art & Design at Suffolk University, Bob has worked for such companies as Disney, Nickelodeon, and Cartoon Network. He lives in North Carolina with his wife Melissa and three children, Will, Charlie, and Mae.